This book belongs to:

_____

AuthorHouse™
1663 Liberty Drive
Bloomington, IN 47403
www.authorhouse.com
Phone: 833-262-8899

Because of the dynamic nature of the Internet, any web addresses or links contained in this book may have changed since publication and may no longer be valid. The views expressed in this work are solely those of the author and do not necessarily reflect the views of the publisher, and the publisher hereby disclaims any responsibility for them.

Any people depicted in stock imagery provided by Getty Images are models, and such images are being used for illustrative purposes only. Certain stock imagery © Getty Images.

This book is printed on acid-free paper.

ISBN: 979-8-8230-0429-9 (sc)
ISBN: 979-8-8230-0430-5 (hc)
ISBN: 979-8-8230-0428-2 (e)

Library of Congress Control Number: 2023905560

Print information available on the last page.

Published by AuthorHouse 05/04/2023

authorHOUSE®

WELCOME TO THE JUNGLE

By Anna M. Donenko

We monkeys think about what we'll do today.

We monkeys like to fool around a bit...
and find plenty of time to eat.

I climb higher,

because

I like the greener,
juiciest leaves.

Our friend the sloth, he's busy today,
but way too slow for us.

Eegads! Better find a safer sandbank.
Our friend the egret needs a better place...

We are out of here!
New place to find...

Great spot, eh?

Let me show you a few
of my bird friends.

a parrot, and a
lovely cotinga.

A toucan,

Look!

9

The hummingbirds are a delightful bunch,
and the beehive, look, but keep some distance!

One of our plans was to have some fun!

Looks like we're stumbling
upon an ant hill.

One of our concerns is the black panther.

Thankfully he prefers to go deeper into the jungle.

WOW! Two capybaras; world's largest rodent.

Mink-a-dink,

Mousey,

and Mr. Frog.

Here's three more pals on the friendly side.

These two butterflies
are seen in great numbers here.
They are originally from Brazil and Peru.

Watch out for the boa, he's full of tricks
as he slithers and slides amongst the sticks.

You might
see an owl.

You might even
see some bats.

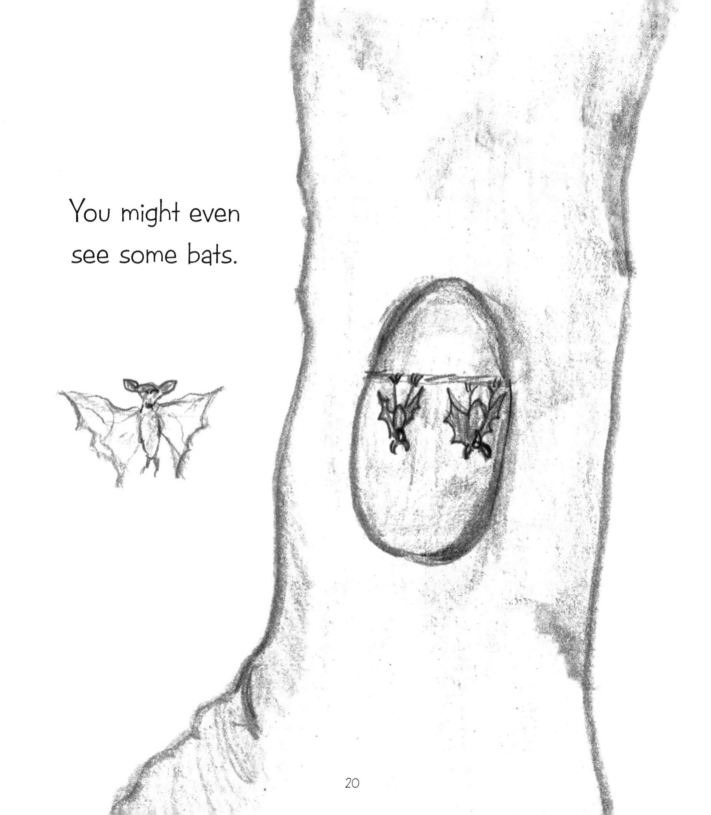

At night you can hear howling and hooting,
But you don't know who's who?

THE END.

Hope you liked touring the jungle with me.

Milton Keynes UK
Ingram Content Group UK Ltd.
UKHW050820300923
429616UK00008B/37